Peter the Caterpillar

Text and Illustrations Copyright © 2015 by Cristina Cabral
Formatting: Gerson Reis
Printed in the USA.

ISBN# 13 978 1515243595

Peter
the
Caterpillar

My deepest gratitude to my dearest friends Nathalia Sutter and Solange Silva, who inspired me to make this story available to others; to my daughters Fernanda and Thais, to Nadia Mattar Went, Mauricio Cisneiros Filho, Roberto Cabral, and all those who supported me through this journey.

This book is dedicated to all of the people in our communities that help make our lives better.

Peter is a Caterpillar. He lives in a tree house with his mom, dad and his sister, Liz. Peter is a good caterpillar, but sometimes he does not listen to his mom when she asks him to pick up his toys.

"Peter, clean up your room," says Mom.
"Later Mom, later," he replies. But usually he forgets to do it.

In the Caterpillar family everyone helps out by doing something. Liz does the dishes and folds the laundry, Dad takes the garbage out and mows the lawn, Mom cleans the house and cooks delicious meals, and Peter... well, Peter always comes up with an excuse to do things later. All he wants is to play, and most of the time he ends up leaving his toys all over the house.

One day, Liz stepped on Peter's favorite car toy and broke its wheel. Peter was furious!

"Liz, look what you did!" he cried.

"I'm sorry Peter!" said Liz. "I didn't see it there. I'm really sorry!"

"I wish I didn't have a sister!" yelled Peter.

"Peter, how many times did I ask you to pick up your toys today?" Mom asked patiently.

"I don't like Liz! I wish I didn't have a sister!" Peter yelled again.

"Oh dear, it is not Liz's fault," said Mom. "Do you think this would have happened if you had put away your toys when you were done playing?"

Peter was so mad that he could not listen to what his Mom was saying.

That night, Peter went to bed angry at Liz. He looked at the moon and wished that he had the world all for himself, so no one could tell him what to do anymore. No more "Pick up your toys" or "Listen to Mom and Dad" or "Use nice words". No more "Be respectful" or "Help each other". He kept looking at the moon and making these wishes until he fell asleep.

The next morning, when Peter woke up the house was very quiet. He went into the kitchen and noticed that there was no breakfast on the table, as there normally was.

"Mom, Dad!" He called. But nobody answered.

"Maybe Liz knows where everybody is," he thought. Peter ran upstairs to Liz's room, but she wasn't there.

"Where is everybody? I need breakfast before I go to school!" he said out loud.

When Peter went to get dressed, he found that all of his clothes were still dirty.

"Really? Nobody did the laundry? How am I going to get dressed for school?"

Peter had no other choice than to go to school in his pajamas. He grabbed an apple to eat on his way to the bus stop, but to his surprise, no one was waiting for the school bus that day. He saw a huge sign on the tree saying "Bus drivers not working today." So, Peter decided to walk to school.

It took him a while to get there.

BUS DRIVERS NOT WORKING TODAY

When Peter finally got to school, the doors were locked and nobody was there. He then, saw another sign saying "Teachers are not working today."

"Oh no! I walked all the way here to find out that there is no school today!" he cried. "Where is everybody? Why is no one working today? Is it a holiday?"

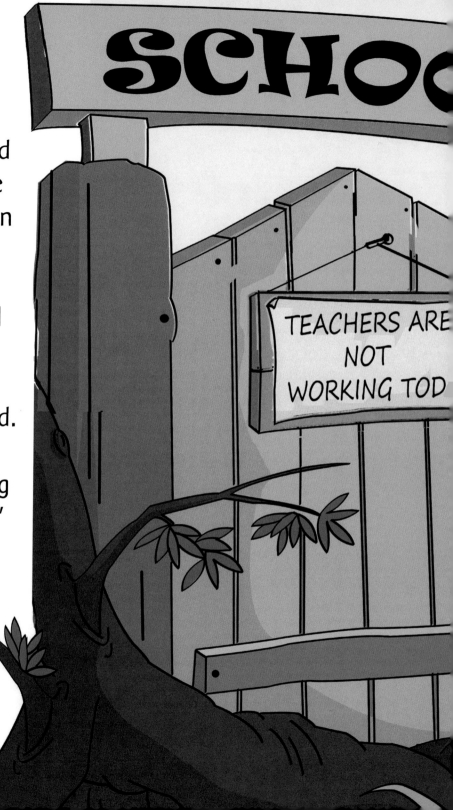

The sun was very hot that day, and Peter was sweating as he walked back home. He decided that he would take a nice cold shower once he got there, but another surprise was waiting for him…

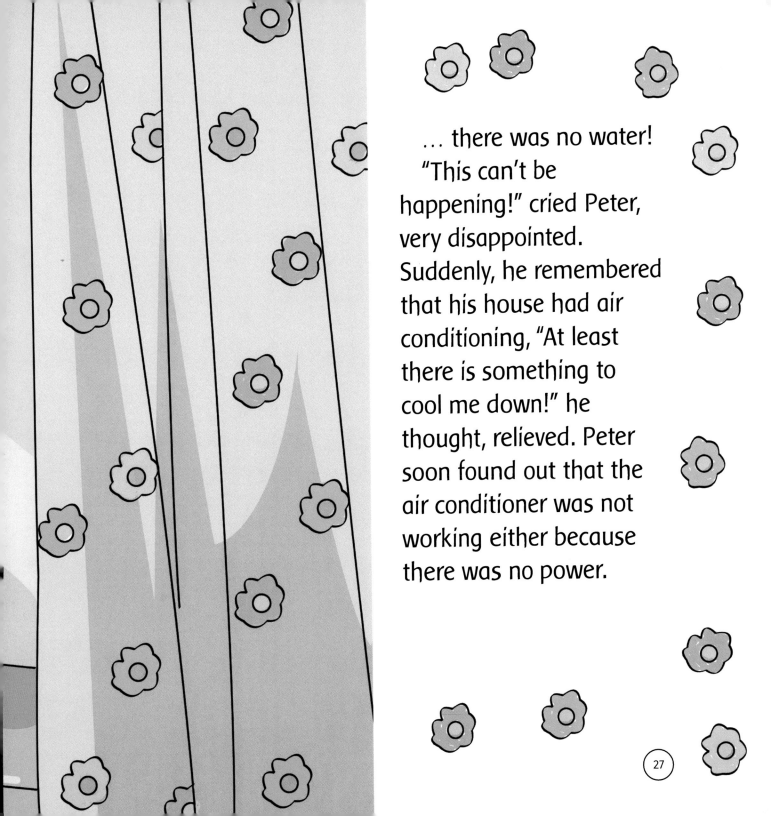

… there was no water! "This can't be happening!" cried Peter, very disappointed. Suddenly, he remembered that his house had air conditioning, "At least there is something to cool me down!" he thought, relieved. Peter soon found out that the air conditioner was not working either because there was no power.

On the kitchen counter there was a note saying, "The power company and the water company are not working today".

"This has to be a joke!" he thought. Peter did not know what to do. He tried to call Grandma, but the phone was not working. "Let me guess," he said to himself, "the phone company is not working today."

Peter looked around. The house was so quiet. He felt very lonely and missed everyone… even Liz. He looked out at the sky and noticed that the day was ending. He could already see the moon.

"What if God decided to stop working? We wouldn't have any more nights, or days, or the moon, or the sun. What if it never rained again? The whole world would be completely dry!"

Peter was worried. In that moment, he realized how God was perfect and created a world filled with people to help one another. He gave us a family to take care of us and help us grow up safely. He also gave us friends, teachers, neighbors, and many other people who make our lives easier.

Before Peter fell asleep, he talked to God in his prayer:

"Dear God, I know I have not been a good son or a good brother lately. Forgive me for not listening to my parents, for not helping them to take care of our home, for being selfish, and also for fighting with Liz. I hope they come back home soon. I miss them so much! I even miss going to school!"

And he fell asleep…

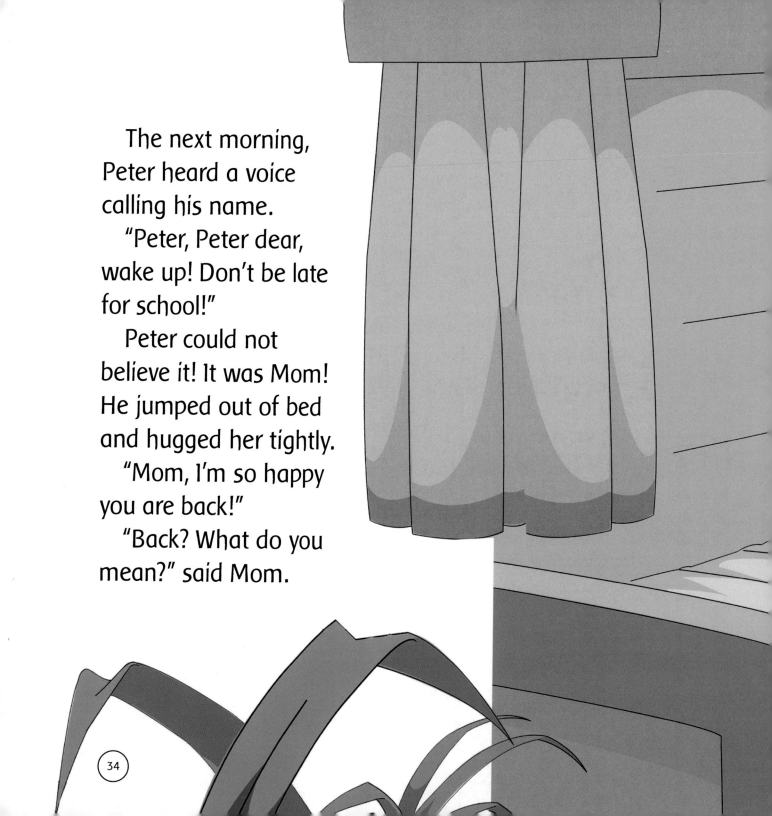

The next morning, Peter heard a voice calling his name.

"Peter, Peter dear, wake up! Don't be late for school!"

Peter could not believe it! It was Mom! He jumped out of bed and hugged her tightly.

"Mom, I'm so happy you are back!"

"Back? What do you mean?" said Mom.